WALKER BOOKS
AND SUBSIDIARIES
LONDON • BOSTON • SYDNEY

First published 1999
by Walker Books Ltd
87 Vauxhall Walk, London SE11 5HJ

10 9 8 7 6 5 4 3 2 1

Text © 1999 Allan Ahlberg
Illustrations © 1999 Paul Howard

This book has been typeset in
Stempel Schneidler Light with
Cafeteria Black.

Printed in Hong Kong

British Library Cataloguing in Publication Data
A catalogue record for this book is
available from the British Library.

ISBN 0-7445-6181-7

For Stanley
P.H.

ALLAN

THE BRAVEST

ILLUSTRATED BY **PAUL**

AHLBERG

EVER BEAR

HOWARD

THE STORIES

The Bear

Once upon a time there was a bear.

That's me!

Huh?

The End

What's going on?

The Other Bear

Once upon a time there was *another* bear.

No, no, it's still me!

The  End

This is no fun.

The Three Bears

Once upon a time there were three bears

– a cottage

– some porridge

– a girl named Goldilocks

– a police chase

– a trial

– and six weeks' community service.

The End

Serves her right!

Once upon a time there were ...

Four and Twenty

Sing a song of sixpence,
A pocketful of rye,

Black Bears

Four and twenty black bears ...
Baked in a pie.

The End

This is ridiculous.

The Penguin

Once upon a time there was a penguin.

A *penguin?*

Yes – what's wrong with penguins?

The End

This is *really* ridiculous!

The Sausage

Once upon a time there was a—

THE BRAVEST

Once upon a time there was a *perfect* bear. When he was a baby he won first prize in the Baby Bear Show. When he went to school he came top of the class. When he grew up he did … hm … lots and lots of very brave things.

He rescued Red Riding Hood – and her grandma – from the Wolf, and tied him up with a skipping-rope until the police came.

Ever Bear

He solved the traffic problem on the Ricketty Racketty Bridge. There was a troll under the bridge. This troll was very big and very hungry. He kept stopping motorists coming back from the supermarket. He threatened to eat them for his supper unless they gave him *all their shopping*.

So people phoned the Bear and asked him to help. Well, what the Bear did was, he punched the Troll on the nose and, just to be sure, he … er … built *another* bridge.

Then one day the Bear did his best and bravest deed of all.

He …

What shall I do?

… slew the Dragon.

The Dragon's picture was in all the newspapers.
He was eating everything – left, right and centre –
and setting fire to things. So the King went on
TV and offered a whole pile of prizes to anyone
who would rid the kingdom of this dreadful dragon.
The prizes included:

a fridge-freezer

a three-piece suite

a Toyota four-wheel drive

and the hand of his daughter in marriage.

After that lots of young men – youngest sons, older brothers, visiting
princes and so on – tried to slay the Dragon and rescue the Princess, whom
the Dragon had previously captured. They came with swords and guns,
horses and bicycles, cars and excavators and fork-lift trucks. But all to no avail.

You can say that again.

The Bear, though, had a better idea. He came …

Help!

with a *fire engine*!

Anyway, in no time at all the Bravest Ever Bear had put that dragon's fire well and truly *out*, rammed him with the engine and tied him up with the hose.

Is your name George?

No.

He didn't actually slay him, though.

After that, the Bear rescued the Princess, collected his prizes, got married and … er … lived happily ever after.

No, he didn't.

The End

No?

No – and it's not the end either.

It's not even the beginning.

It's the *wrong* story!

Anyway, I'm not marrying a *bear*.

How about a penguin?

Push off, Penguin!

Now, let's see...

The Perfectest

Once upon a time there was a princess.

I thought this was a bear book.

This princess was the fairest in the land
– *of course* – but also smart.
She had no trouble with dragons, trolls
or wolves, come to that.

Really?

And no time for princes.

Push off, Prince!

Aaargh !

Ever Princess

Also, she was just sick of footmen and French maids – gardeners and grooms – governesses – homework – keeping her room tidy – not having her own TV – *princes* (I mentioned them already!) and … palace life altogether. So, one day what she did was, she … er … let's see … she moved into a flat with a couple of friends, started a career in television – and went shopping.

The End

Push off, Prince!

Aaargh !

The End?

I doubt it.

You can say that again. We've hardly …

STA

I don't like this book.

Oo-er!

R T E D!

Now, let's see...

The Wolf, the Troll

Once upon a time there was a happy wolf. All day long he just sat around eating little pigs (three at a time), little girls, baskets of shopping, grandmas and so on.

His best pal was a troll. He ate baskets of shopping too – and shoppers. Often the Wolf and the Troll would have little snacks under the Troll's comfortable and cosy bridge.

Or they would go on a picnic.

and the Dragon

One day the Wolf and the Troll were out with their picnic basket
when who should they meet but their other old pal, the Dragon.
The Dragon was in a dreadful state. He had just been
run over, believe it or not, by a *bear in a fire engine*!
This bear was well-known to the Wolf and the Troll.

Was he?

They had had trouble with him themselves.
So then what these three loyal companions –
musketeers, you might call them –
what they did was, they
straight away went down
into the town and
got their own back.

**All for one and
one for all!**

In the town there was a king and queen,
a bride and groom, a wedding

Ah!   **Not this again!**

and a *banquet*.   **Hooray!**

Also a wolf, a troll and a dragon,

That's us!   who just came strolling in …

and ate the lot!

The **BURP!** End

Pardon me!

No, no, you forgot one thing...

The Wedding Cake

Oh yes, the cake! Well, then – surprise, surprise! –
out of the cake jumped four and twenty
black bears – black *belt* bears, actually.
In next to no time they had wrestled the
Wolf, the Troll and the Dragon into
a submission, and tied them up.

Everybody cheered. The King was so
pleased that he gave the bears half his
kingdom and a twenty-four-piece suite.
So then, of course, the banquet could continue.
The trouble was there *was* no banquet.
Not a crumb. Not a drop. Not a sausage.
There again, speaking
of sausages…

The Sausage

Huh?

Once upon a time there was a sausage, *there was,* there really was. This sausage was a chef. *As it happened,* he had cooked the first banquet (and the first cake).

So all he had to do … was cook another.

Nothing to it.

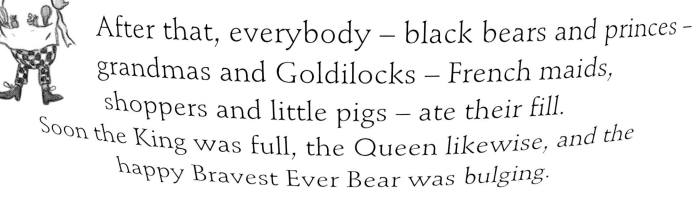

After that, everybody – black bears and *princes* – grandmas and Goldilocks – French maids, shoppers and little pigs – ate their fill. Soon the King was full, the Queen *likewise, and the* happy Bravest Ever Bear was *bulging.*

The End

Put me to bed
but don't
bend me.

The Bed

Once upon a time there was a bed

Good!

with a bear in it.

Better still.

The End

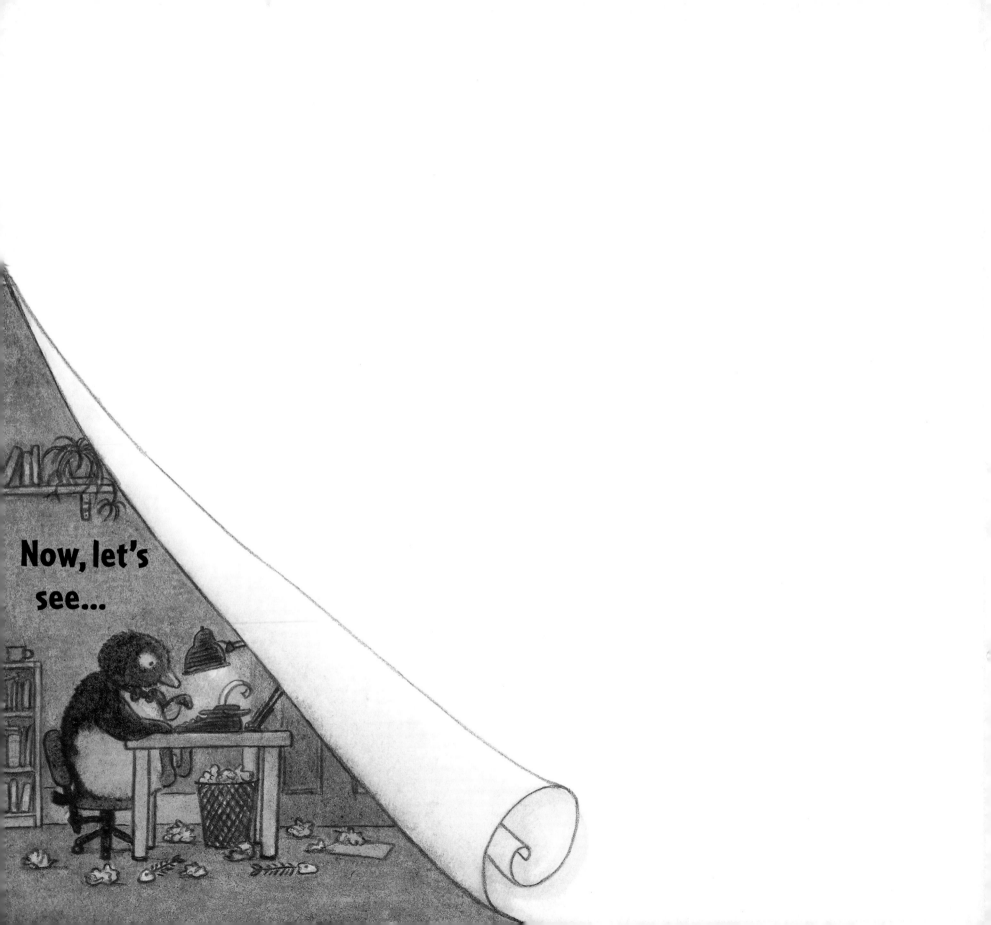

Now, let's see...